PENGUIN BOOKS

DULCIMA

Born in 1905, H. E. Bates was educated at Kettering Grammar School and worked as a journalist before publishing his first book, *The Two Sisters*, when he was twenty. In the next fifteen years he won a distinguished reputation for his stories about English country life. In 1941, as 'Flying Officer X', he wrote his two famous books of short stories – *The Greatest People in the World* and *How Sleep the Brave* – which were followed in 1944 by *Fair Stood the Wind for France*. These, and his subsequent novels of Burma, *The Purple Plain* and *The Jacaranda Tree*, and of India, *The Scarlet Sword*, stemming directly or indirectly from his war experience in the East, won him a new reputation and, apart from their success in Britain and America, have been translated into sixteen foreign languages. His writing took a new direction with the appearance in 1958 of *The Darling Buds of May*, the first of the popular Larkin family novels, which was followed by *A Breath of French Air*, *When the Green Woods Laugh*, and *Oh! To be in England* (1963). *A Lover's Flowers* (1971) is his most recent book.

H. E. BATES

Dulcima

PENGUIN BOOKS
IN ASSOCIATION WITH
MICHAEL JOSEPH

Penguin Books Ltd, Harmondsworth, Middlesex, England
Penguin Books Australia Ltd, Ringwood, Victoria, Australia

—

The collection *The Nature of Love*, containing *Dulcima*,
first published by Michael Joseph 1953
Published in Penguin Books 1958
Dulcima reissued as a separate volume in Penguin Books 1971

—

Made and printed in Great Britain
by Hazell Watson & Viney Ltd,
Aylesbury, Bucks
Set in Linotype Juliana

To
W. SOMERSET MAUGHAM

1

SHE was a short girl, thick in the back, with stout legs covered by brownish cotton stockings and flat feet by big sloppy shoes. Her hands were large and coarse and her straight dark hair hung down over her solid cheek-bones in uncombed strands. In twenty-seven years she had never had much time, as she remembered it, to bother with her hair.

Every afternoon she pushed an old hoodless pram, with a baby in it, up the hillside, through high woods of beeches, under greening crags of chalk, to where the road ended by Parker's farm. The woods were so large that there were always new-blown branches of beechwood lying on the slopes of dry copper leaves and she always loaded the pram with them, so that finally the baby lay almost buried under a crooked roof of boughs. When she pushed the pram up the road she thrust her head forward, making the big solid legs dig backwards and gain their power from the slope of the hill. When she went down the hill she thrust her legs forward, straining the front of her body outward, so that she could hold the load from running away. Sometimes after storms the woods were filled with a wreckage of broken branches and she felt greedy about it and piled the pram so high with them that she could hardly hold the weight of it back. Then she ran down the hill, pounding her thick legs on the road with lumbering stabs that filled the long high woods with clapping echoes.

She was very conscious of her legs; she had always been terribly aware of their ugliness. She was aware too of the coarseness of her hands. But she felt that she could have borne even the ugliness of the big squabby hands and the flabbiness of a face in which the lips were too thick and the eyes slightly out of proportion and the hair too coarse to bother with if only her legs had been tolerable. Every girl wanted legs with some kind of shapeliness. There were things you could do to a plain or even an ugly face to make it more tolerable, even to make it attractive or striking or beautiful, and you could always put smooth new gloves on your hands. But she felt there was nothing you could do to change legs that were only lumps of fat hideously knotted with raised blue veins. They were something horrible, like a deformity, an affliction, you could not disguise.

She felt too that there were reasons why her legs had grown like that. She had never known the time when there was not a baby in the pram. She had never known the time when she was not slopping up the hill in her big flat shoes, pushing the pram, covering it with firewood, then pushing it down again. There seemed never to have been a time when she did not stand at the copper, pounding at clothes, or at the sink, washing dishes for a dozen people. She knew that these were the things that thickened and coarsened and twisted your legs into shapelessness, tying them with slaty and hideous veins. Standing and lugging and standing and pushing and standing on

8

her own weight all day had destroyed the things she wanted to be most beautiful.

Her mother was a hollow-faced whining woman with meagre breasts that were like empty purses except when they filled briefly and fed another child. Her face was yellow with a haunted look. It was the look of someone trying to remember something – a pleasant thing or a comforting thing or the reason for something or the details of a lost intention. She seemed to be trying to recapture something. And over the years she had expressed the impossibility of recapture by giving her children proud and fancy names. They were called Rowena and Chalice and Spenser, and then Clarissa and Angela and Cassandra and Abigail, and even Magnolia and Sharon, two who had died.

The name of the eldest, the girl who pushed the pram, was Dulcima. Her father called her Dulce. It was her mother's way, in preservation of successive dreams, to call the children by their full names, with a kind of round, doting, stupid grandeur. But for her father it was Dulce. It was Abb and Cass and Clar and Ange and even Ro and Spen. Her father, a man with cheeks fissured dark by long hours in brick kilns, had no time for names, for doting or for fanciful things. Work at the kiln seemed, after years, to have burnt the juices out of him, so that he was dry of kindliness. Shallow grey eyes were cemented into a head that had no colour. Even the diminutives of the names he used were not soft in effect. He rapped them out hard and chipped, like chisel blows.

'Drop that, Abb, else I'll git the strap. Stoppit, Cass –

any more lip and I'll mark you. I'll mark you, by God I will.'

He was proud, as he said, to have them at a word.

'I want shoes,' she would say. 'I'm walking wet-foot now. I bin walking wet-foot for a week. Every day.'

'You'll git shoes, you'll git shoes. I ain't made o' shoes, am I?'

'Git shoes with what? They had a pair at the jumble and I hadn't a mite to bless myself with. Git shoes with what?'

'Dulcima, don't you urge your father. Don't you urge him like that –'

'Let him git me a pair o' shoes then. Let him stop Dulcing me all day long. Dulce this, Dulce that, where's Dulce? Let him stop Dulcing me and git me a pair o' shoes.'

'You'll git shoes, time enough, you'll git shoes.'

'Time enough for what? – I'll git shoes but it won't be here. I'll Dulce out o' here one o' these days. I'll Dulce out and git myself some shoes. I ain't a dog walking on my bare feet. I ain't a dog – I won't be treated like a dog.'

Like a dog, every afternoon, she pushed the pram through the beechwoods, up the hill. Like her mother, as she pressed forward on thick ugly legs, she became pre-occupied with successive dreams: a dream of shoes, of a decent dress, a dream of some way to make her legs less hideous, of a time when she might wear white gloves on her hands.

2

EVERY Tuesday and Friday, market days, Parker came up the hill, driving a mud-stained open Ford with a trailer.

She did not think of this as an extraordinary thing. It happened so regularly and so often that she hardly noticed it. Always on those days, about the same time, she heard the clash of gears as Parker turned the corner and began to climb the hill through the beeches. She heard the echoed rattle of the worn-out Ford clashing up into the high cover of branches. She saw the car coming out of the lower woodland like a drugged and slightly crazy buffalo, nosing from side to side, lurching in heavy curves so that sometimes she had to pull the pram into the chalk verge until it was safely past her.

Every day too she saw the thin drunk-grey face of Parker as it went past without looking at her. In winter mud from the Ford splashed her cotton stockings and as spring came on white chalk dust was beaten up into her face. She showed no sign that these things irritated her. Sometimes she stood holding a broken branch in her hand, staring thoughtfully after Parker, watching him until, at last, the car lurched and disappeared through the gate of the farm.

One day in late April Parker came up the hill faster than usual. She heard the car roaring up the road like an ancient and rickety train. She had just time to pull the pram into the verge before Parker went past her and the Ford, bouncing, hit the snake fence thirty yards beyond.

At first she did not move. She stood gripping the handle of the pram and watching Parker trying to get out of the car. She saw the drunk-grey face straining across the seats; the hands groping along the edges of the dusty car body for support.

She watched for some moments longer and then Parker fell out of the car. He hit the roadside face first and then turned over convulsively and lay still. At the same moment the car engine coughed in a back-fire that was like a pistol-shot and the sound woke the baby, so that it began to cry. The sound of its crying startled her more than the crash had done and suddenly she found herself running forward, shouting:

'Mr Parker! Mr Parker! Are you all right, Mr Parker? Whatever has happened?'

After some moments Parker opened his eyes, saw her and tried to stand up. She watched him for some seconds shuddering on the raised edge of grass. Then he fell down on his face again. His black trilby hat had already fallen off and now she picked it up. It was covered with a white bloom of chalk dust and she began to brush it with her hands.

The inner rim of the hat, when she turned it over, seemed to be stuffed with paper: as if it were too big for the small skinny head of Parker, who had padded it to the right size.

Then she saw that this paper was not merely paper. It was in the form of many pound notes, neatly folded and packed tight inside the hat, under the greasy leather band.

'I'll get you home, Mr Parker,' she said. 'Mr Parker, I'll get you home.'

For some few seconds she was torn between the problem of Parker, the hat, and the crying baby. She solved it by leaving Parker where he was and taking the hat to the pram. Then she pushed the pram to the farm-gate, rocking it up and down so that the baby stopped its crying. Finally she pushed the hat behind the pillow and then came back to where Parker was.

He was still dazed as she lifted him up with stout arms and, in the same solid way as she pushed the pram up and down the hill, carried him to the house. His fall had left a long streak of blood on his left cheek and she said:

'Mr Parker, you might have killed yourself,' but Parker did not answer.

After she had dumped Parker into the big horsehair chair in the kitchen, her first thought was for the hat. She wheeled the pram to the kitchen door and then took out the hat and put it on the kitchen table.

'I'll git you a cuppa tea, Mr Parker,' she said. 'I'll wash that blood off your face and git you a cuppa tea and you'll feel better.'

Again Parker did not answer. Nor did he seem to notice her movements about the kitchen as she filled the kettle, lighted the oil stove and got ready to bathe his face and make the tea. Cups and plates that Parker had used in the morning or the day before or even the day before that stood about the kitchen in odd places, on chairs, on the mantelshelf, on window-ledges, in a sink filled with greasy stewpans.

'You let yourself git into a rare mess,' she said and began to bathe his face.

Parker was a man of fifty-five and she had always thought of him, when she had thought of him at all, as being older than he was. Her first close look at his face did not change her mind. It was a face of small bone structure, narrow, with thin lips and sparse receding rabbit-coloured hair. A little frown of pained anxiety about something brought the small grey eyes rather close together.

Some time after she had washed his face Parker sat up. With stupefied eyes he looked glassily past her. He sat staring in this way until she brought him tea. She had the sense to bring it to him without a saucer and he sat with the cup grasped in both hands, staring, letting the tea fume up into his washed grey face without a word.

'Feel any better?' she said. 'You might have got yourself killed,' but again Parker did not answer.

While he drank the tea, she looked at the floor, splashed with grey hen-droppings, with mud and mud-straw from the yard and with old stray feathers; at the crockery lying on mantelpiece and window-sill and chairs; and at the colourless skeins of lace that had once been curtains; and she said:

'Don't nobody come in and give you a clean-up once in a while?'

He seemed to shake his head; and suddenly she felt in a clumsy way sorry for him: drunk, womanless, lost, unable to answer her.

'Well, it's time somebody did.' She pulled at her stockings that had slipped slightly down in concertina ruckles over her stout legs, but Parker did not notice them. 'If I git time tomorrow I'll come in and give you a bit of a sweep-up. Not afore you want it either.'

Parker seemed to nod his head, still as if not seeing her properly, and after some moments she said, 'You take care of yourself, Mr Parker, you'll be killing yourself one o' these days,' and then she lumbered out into the yard and pushed the baby down the hill.

3

WHEN she came up the hill on the following afternoon it was with the thought of Parker, rather than the hat, uppermost in her mind. She did not conceive the hat as an important thing. Spring was coming across the valley and puffs of blossom, like tranquil smoke, rose everywhere about the pastures below the hill. Under a sharp blue sky the beeches were brilliant masses of almost transparent lace-like leaf and it puzzled her, almost irked her, that a man could live as Parker lived in the spring time: womanless, unswept, curtains unwashed, the old crust of winter still clinging everywhere like a frowsy mould.

So she was glad to see Parker waiting for her by the gate; she was glad to see him looking in so many ways different from the day before. His face was clean and its drunken greyness had gone; he was no longer wearing his best black hat. He was a little working farmer in shirt sleeves, still too narrow of face, too pin-eyed and too cautious, but human and aware.

'How d'you feel today, Mr Parker?'

'Ain't so bad.'

'Was your car hurt?'

'It's all right.'

'I said I'd give you a bit of a clean-up but I got to git back by four,' she said. 'How if I came in for hour after tea? I could come up.'

'You pick my hat up yesterday?' he said.

'Yes, Mr Parker,' she said. 'I picked it up. I put it in the kitchen.'

'Oh,' he said.

'You never lost nothing, did you?' she said.

'Not as I know on,' Parker said.

She stood by the pram, rocking the baby up and down, talking a little more, and after a time Parker watched her go back through the wood. When she came back soon after six o'clock, without the baby, Parker was not there. She could hear the sound of a tractor down the hill.

The evening was very warm and soft and a deep fragrance of bluebells came from hazel copses above the house as she turned the kitchen furniture into the farmyard and then took the curtains from the windows and hung them, like disintegrating cobwebs, on the clothes line. She scrubbed the kitchen floor, the stove, and the stone steps outside. Water ran like mud, bearing away with it the stale rank odours of old grease, old cooking, old dust, and the curious close stench of winter decay. She washed up the crockery of the past week and opened the windows and let in the spring evening air.

When she had finished all this she walked into the yard to look for Parker. When she could not see him she walked across to a small orchard beyond the cow-barn. Down the hill Parker was harrowing ground for spring seed. The soil was dry and dusty and the tractor seemed to draw behind it a brown and smoky cloud.

Everywhere primroses, with drifts of white anemone, were growing in lush masses under hazel-trees and she gathered a handful while she waited for Parker to come in with the harrow. But after a time there seemed to be something wrong with the tractor and she gave up waiting and went back into the house.

She put the primroses into a little red glass jug on the supper table. She had already laid out all the food she could find, a little bread, a piece of home-killed bacon, and a lump of cheese. Now she sat down to wait for Parker and after about ten minutes he came in.

For some moments he stood on the kitchen threshold with small rabbity eyes transfixed by all he saw. This transfixed narrow stare was not surprised or unbelieving or even doubtful. It was held in suspicion: as if he could not accept it without also accepting that behind it there lay some sort of motive. Nobody did such things for nothing; nobody gave things away without wanting something back.

'I didn't have much time, Mr Parker,' she said, 'but it's a bit better. It's a bit sweeter anyway.'

'Ah,' he said.

'I don't know what you want for supper,' she said. 'That's all I could forage. I'll make you a cuppa tea.'

While she was in the scullery making tea Parker sat at the table in concentration on the food, gnawing with slow greed at lumps of bread.

'You want some new curtains,' she said. 'Them others'll fall to pieces if you wash 'em.'

'I got no money for curtains.'

'Well, it's your place,' she said. 'You wanta look after it.'

'I ain't made o' money,' he said. 'I got a living to git.'

For a second or two it occurred to her to say something about the money in the hat; thirty or forty pounds of it, something that seemed extraordinarily vast to her. It seemed not only incredible but also idiotic that anyone with so much money tucked into the brim of his hat could speak so narrowly and meanly as Parker did. Such dreams as lay in the brim of Parker's hat were stupendous. They were dreams she had often thought about and had never attained.

She said simply instead: 'I'll just pour myself a cup and then run along or else somebody'll be in a two-and-eight at home.'

He drew lumps of pork gristle from his mouth and dropped them on the new-scrubbed floor.

'What's your name?' he said.

'Gaskain.'

'One o' Jim Gaskain's lot?'

'Yes.'

'Which one are you?'

'Dulcima,' she said.

For the first time he smiled. This smile seemed no more than a bristling of dirty teeth from between thin greasy lips, but she was wholly aware of it. It seemed to humanize Parker a little further.

'Funny name, ain't it?' Parker said. 'What do they call you?'

'Dulcie,' she said. 'Or else Dulce.'

'Worse 'n Dulcima,' he said.

She did not answer. She had been a little sorry for Parker; she had been a little puzzled and baffled by him; and now she was hurt. It seemed a poor return for her kindness, and deep down in her there was kindled, for the first time, out of the terse and narrow uncharitableness about her name, a remote spark of resentment.

'Well, I'll be going now,' she said.

He guzzled tea. She waited at the door for a word of acknowledgement, of thanks, of simple recognition, for the things she had done, but he did not speak and she said:

'How about them curtains? I could git the stuff for you if you wanted.'

'I'll atta see.'

'Everybody says they're goin' up again,' she said. 'You could save a bit now.'

'Ah?'

'You could save ten or twelve shillings,' she said. 'Very like more. You could be twelve or thirteen shillings in pocket.'

'Ah?' he said. He appeared to consider this possibility; it seemed to appeal to him. Then the sudden touch of humanity that made her feel inexplicably sorry for him came out again:

'Ain't had no new curtains since the missus died.'

'Then it's time you had some,' she said. 'You let me git 'em and fix 'em up.'

He hesitated for some moments longer, and then:

'All right,' he said. 'You git 'em.'

He spoke flatly, staring at the primroses, as if seeing them for the first time.

'I shall want some money,' she said.

'All right,' he said. 'I'll atta see about that.'

*

After that she began to go up to the farm every evening. With the money Parker gave her she bought the material for the curtains and made them and hung them up. They were of bright yellow material, with scrolling scarlet roses, and they flapped like signal flags against the windows of the square drab house on the hill. As summer came on she cleaned through the sitting-room, the stairs and the landing, and then into the three bedrooms above. Parker had slept in a small back bedroom on an iron bedstead, throwing an old army overcoat over himself for extra warmth in winter. She turned him out of this frowsy unwashed room into another and then out of that into another, until the three were cleaned. She beat the dust from the carpets in the farmyard and washed the sheets until they too looked like long rows of signal flags strung out under the summer apple-trees.

From time to time Parker said 'I shall atta settle for your time,' or 'Soon as I git that hayin' done I'll settle up wi' you,' but on all these occasions she would simply look at him with her slow dark eyes, as if searching for something beyond him, and say:

'It don't matter. There's no hurry, Mr Parker. There's plenty of time.'

Summer was dry and beautiful on the hill and in the evenings, from that high point about the farm, the sun seemed to go down very slowly across the plain of deep flat country below. Because of this she got into the habit of waiting for Parker to come in from the fields, no matter how late it was. Now that the rooms were all turned out and tidy it was easier to keep everything clean and sometimes there was nothing to do but lay the table for supper.

While she waited she got into the habit of sitting at the kitchen table and writing down, in a small black notebook, a little account of all the things she had done. She wrote very simply. She wrote down: 'Mr Parker, April 24th, 1½ hrs, 2/3; Mr Parker, curtain pins and tape, 7/6; Mr Parker, June 8, 2½ hrs, 3/9; Mr Parker, soap and scrubbing brush, 3/6; Mr Parker, making curtains, 16/6.' At the bottom of each page she added up the figure and carried it over to the next. Sometimes she checked it over for a mistake and when she heard Parker coming in from the fields she stuffed the book down between the front of her body and her dress. In that way it made no difference to the solid stoutness of her figure, squabby and shapeless from her bust down to the heavy plodding legs still covered with cotton stockings.

Every Tuesday and Friday Parker came home from market, driving wildly up the hill. She grew so used to it that after a time she got into the habit of going up to the farm a little earlier on those days so that she could take off his shoes where he had fallen on the kitchen floor, and loosen his collar and find his hat. There was always money in the hat, twenty or thirty pounds, and once, after some heifer calves had been sold, fifty or sixty; but she did not touch it. It was as if she did not regard the debt that Parker owed her as having any bearing on this; as if something in Parker or something in herself, his meanness and her own patience, were quite separate, and as if she could wait for a long time, perhaps years, before they came together.

By July summer began to burn the thin earth of the hillside until the chalk was like dry white flame and there was an evening in late July when she found it too hot to sit in the kitchen. Instead she sat on the stone steps outside, writing her accounts in the small black book, her cotton stockings rolled down, for coolness, over her ankles.

That evening Parker came unexpectedly from the barn behind the house, surprising her. She was torn for a moment between the necessity of hiding the book and the necessity of rolling up her stockings, and she decided on the book. Some moments later Parker was crossing the threshold, stepping over her thick bare legs as he went into the house for supper.

'Everything's on the table,' she said. 'I'll be there in a minute.'

She stretched out her big fleshy legs and began to roll up her stockings and Parker, at the kitchen table, sat watching her.

He watched her for some time longer, across the table, as he ate his meal. Heat came in pulsating thick waves as it rose from the valley. Once again she began to long for a breath of air and suddenly she decided, a little earlier than usual, to get up and go.

As she reached the doorway Parker got up from the table, his eyes curiously excited, and said:

'How about you coming up here for good?' he said. 'I bin wanting to ask you.'

'Me?' she said. 'No.'

'Ah, come on,' he said. 'You like it up here. Don't you like it?'

'I like it.'

'You come up and keep house for me. I'll pay. When you finished in the house you can give me a hand outside. I'll pay.'

'I couldn't,' she said.

'I'll pay.'

'I couldn't.'

'Why?' he said. 'Why? I git on well with you. I'll pay.'

'Oh! I don't know,' she said. It was as if she seemed to give way a little, to consider it. She looked past him with black slow eyes, in remote calculation. 'You keep saying pay but how do I know? What'll you pay?'

'Two pound,' he said. 'And keep.' It was like speaking of an animal. 'Two pound a week.'

'I could get that down in the village. Without traipsing all this naughty way up here.'

She lied flatly, calmly, as if for some time she had prepared herself for it.

'All right. Two pounds ten.'

'Then there's what you owe me.'

'I know, I know that,' he said. Clumsily he tried to grasp her shoulders but she held herself back, pressed against the doorpost. 'I bin meaning – you didn't think I wadn't goin' to pay, Dulcie, did you? Eh? You didn't think –'

'You'll pay,' she said. 'I know.'

'You come then,' he said, 'will you? Eh? It'll be all right? Two pounds ten, eh?'

'I got to think it over. There's –'

'What?' he said. 'There's what?'

'There's a lot of things. Well, there's other people –'

'Ah,' he said. He could not guess now at what she was thinking; she simply gave the impression of holding something back.

'I'll tell you tomorrow,' she said.

When she came back, next day, in the early evening, she was surprised to find him already home from the fields. He had changed his shirt and had put on a clean celluloid collar, high and rather old-fashioned, with a brown clip-on tie.

'You think about what I said?' he asked her.

'A bit.'

'You'll come then, will you? Eh?'

She did not answer; for some time she walked about the kitchen, and then into the scullery and back again, getting his tea. He began to follow her, dog-like, his face in its scrubbed cleanness queerly earnest above the high choking collar.

'It ain't bad up here, is it? You like it, don't you?'

'Yes, but what am I going to do with myself all day? Nobody to talk to – nobody up here.'

'I'll take you into town – market days, Saturdays – no need to be lonely –'

'It ain't that.'

She seemed to dispose of one objection and then suddenly, flatly, emotionlessly, bring up another.

'It ain't only what I think,' she said.

'Who else then? Your dad?'

'No,' she said. 'I don't care about him.'

'Who else then?'

'Well – there's somebody.'

'Who?' he said. 'Who?'

'My boy. My young man.'

'Never knowed you had one.'

'You don't know everything, do you?' she said.

He sat at the table, not answering, confused and very quiet. He stared down at her strong thick legs and then up at her arms. The flesh of her arms, for all its plumpness, was fine and smooth and now in high summer it gleamed a strong soft brown from sun.

'Don't think he'd want you to?' he said.

'Well, I got to think about him, haven't I?' she said. 'I got to consider him.'

'What's his name?'

'Albert.'

She spoke readily, lying again about the name as she had already lied about the young man himself and as yesterday she had lied about the village and the money. It was as if she wanted to fire in Parker a terrible and foolish eagerness; and then in turn to break down, by a series of little things, the caution in him that had once conceived her as a trap.

'You think he wouldn't like it?' he said.

'It ain't only that.'

'What else is it?'

She lied again: 'He gives me a few shillings a week,' she said. 'Saving money. So we can git a few things ready. So we can be married some day.'

'Married?' he said. The eagerness in him, already roused, seemed to split his eyes with small fires of helpless bewilderment. 'You goin' git married?'

'Well, some day I hope.'

'Three pound a week,' he said. 'If I give you that, will you come?'

Once again she looked beyond him with her small dark eyes.

'I'll ask Albert tonight,' she said. 'He'll probably murder me.'

4

WHEN she moved in, two days later, with all her belong-
ings packed in a cheap brown fibre suit-case, she gave
Parker the impression not that it was something she
had long prepared but that it was something she was
doing with his own peculiar caution, as a favour,
reluctantly.

'I'll try it for a week,' she said. 'I'll give it a trial.'

She moved into the front bedroom and at night she
locked her door. She made a point, during those first few
days, of speaking often of Albert. She wondered what
Albert would say if he could see her now; she wondered
what on earth she would do if Albert popped in. Albert
came gradually forward into the situation not simply as a
third party but as a watchful and terrifying eye, keeping
guard on her. She brought him along as a person of possessive and jealous desire. Albert was a terror for getting
to know everything: you couldn't keep anything from
Albert. Whatever she did Albert got to know. Albert
would brain her if she didn't do this and didn't do that.
There was no fooling Albert.

On the following Tuesday she and Parker drove down
to market together for the first time.

'I only hope we don't see Albert,' she said. 'I had to kid
him with all sorts of tales about you.'

Parker felt pleased at this. In his ignorance of her lying
he was flattered.

'Never mind about Albert. You keep along o' me,' he said. 'I got a few fly deals on today.'

Throughout the day Parker went about the market like a nosing fox. She had grown used to the fact that, up at the farm, he sometimes did not speak much. Now he hardly spoke at all. Now whatever he was thinking seemed to become locked up. The dumb grey eyes flickered occasionally in a tight-drawn face that otherwise had no expression. He leaned on cow-stalls, making bargains, staring at dung-splashed concrete, eyes downcast. She saw him for the first time as a person of ruthless and one-track brain, scheming and cunning, lying too, fanatically pursuing one end. And gradually, beside him, her own thoughts and her own lying seemed very little, quite innocent, of no serious account at all.

During most of that time he did not notice her. Somewhere about noon he went into the *Market Arms* to start the first drinking of the day. She went away alone and bought herself a dinner of roast beef and potatoes and apple tart and afterwards a cup of tea in a back-street dining-rooms. While she drank the tea she wrote in her little book: 'Dinner. July 15. 3/4.'

After that, about two o'clock, she went back to find Parker. She found him drinking, but not drunk; and she pulled nervously at his sleeve:

'Mr Parker, I just seen Albert. I don't know whether he seen me or not but I'm scared of what he'll do.'

'We'd better git home.'

'That's what I thought,' she said.

And once again Parker, because of what she said about Albert, was pleased. It flattered him greatly to think that she was afraid of Albert for his sake. He drove home with a smile on his face and a little more caution than usual: a good day, a hat full of money and now, on top of it, they were kidding Albert. They were running away from Albert together.

In this way they lived for three or four weeks, through July and into harvest. On the hill the summer had been very hot, almost rainless, scorching the barley straw so that it was short, no higher than white grass, and easy to gather. Besides herself Parker had no help except a part-time hand, an oldish man named Barnes, and the three of them worked at the small harvest together.

One afternoon Barnes stopped working and stood staring down the hillside; then he walked forward across the stubble a yard or two and squinted.

'Somebody a-prowlin' about down there,' he said. 'Somebody with a gun.'

'Oh!' she said.

'Where's that?' Parker said.

'Down aside the bottom gate,' Barnes said. 'Young chap. I can see the gun.'

'It looks like Albert,' she said.

After a time the young man with the gun disappeared, and once again Parker got the feeling that he had done very well for himself. Not merely was she a good girl, a willing girl, a hard-working girl; she was a girl that someone else wanted. The thought of Albert jealous, Albert prowling about with a gun, Albert watching her, was something that puffed him with satisfaction.

That evening she was changing in her room when Parker went past on the landing. Her door was open a little. She had taken off her dress and she was stooping over her attaché case, which lay open on the bed.

Parker opened the door slightly and looked in. 'Was wondering where you were,' he said.

'I'm just changing,' she said.

He saw the attaché case open on the bed.

'Ain't goin' nowheres, are you?' he said.

'Oh! I don't know,' she said. 'I don't know. I get worried.'

'Worried?' he said. He came into the bedroom. 'Here, what's this?'

'Well, it's Albert,' she said. 'It's Albert.' She began quickly brushing her hair as if she were nervous, almost a little distracted. 'When people start prowling about with guns I think it's time I got back home –'

'No,' he said. 'Don't do that.'

He came over to her and put his arms across her bare shoulders, clumsily. He began to seem a little distracted too, troubled by the thought of losing her.

'God, no,' he said. 'Don't do that, Dulcie, you can't do that.'

'I can if Albert says so.'

She gave her hair a long deep casual stroke with the brush. That summer, for the first time in her life, she had found time to spend on her hair, and now it brushed out into a thick black fringe that fell over his hands. As she tossed it back again, the dark hair falling over her white plump shoulder, her big breast was strained upward. In a tortured and clumsy way he struggled for a few moments to thrust himself nearer her body, and she pushed him away.

32

'Here, steady, we're not married.'

'I don't want you to go –'

'Yes, but people prowling about with guns. Besides,' she said suddenly, 'you ain't paid me –'

'I know. I'll pay,' he said. 'I'll pay.'

'You keep saying that.'

'I'll pay,' he said. 'I'll pay tonight. I'll git it after supper.'

'All of it?'

'Yeh,' he said. 'Yeh. All on it. I'll pay.'

'All right,' she said. 'You git it after supper. I'll reckon how much it is.'

She brushed her hair once again with long, casual, and now almost contemptuous swinging of the brush; she brought it down in a black arch over her sun-brown face, tossed it away again, bringing up the arch of her plump white shoulder.

'Don't look so miserable,' she said. 'I ain't gone yet.'

'Don't go,' he said. 'I wouldn't want you to go.'

After supper he got up from the table, looking round with troubled rabbity eyes.

'You want me to pay you now?'

'I could do with it,' she said.

'How much d'ye reckon it'll be?'

'I don't know exactly. I got it all down somewheres,' she said, 'in my room. You git the money. I'll be up there. It ain't so much.'

She spoke casually, off-hand, as if now, after all, the money did not matter. She looked at his furtive face and she saw that he was past being troubled and was almost frightened. Then she recalled his face as she had seen it in

33

the market, making his deals, unrelaxed and relentless, the face of a dumb fox, and it almost surprised her to see now, at last, how excruciating the change in him was.

She went up to her room. She did not look at the little book. Instead she lay full length on the bed, listening, looking at the blue August evening sky, turning the figure in the book over and over in her mind: twenty-one pounds five-and-six, twenty-one pounds five-and-six, twenty-one –

All this time she could hear Parker lumbering in the attic above her head. She had never been up to the attic. A little flight of wooden steps led up to it and the door was always locked. What was up there she did not know but she felt that perhaps soon, now, there would be ways of knowing. She could persuade Parker, perhaps, to tell her what was there. Twenty-one pounds – did it matter what was in the little book? Did it matter to a pound, one way or another? Twenty-four pounds, twenty-seven? Need Parker know? She stared dreaming at the August sky, still quivering with the heat of the day, and decided that Parker need never know.

When at last he came down from the attic and she heard him shuffling in the corridor outside she called:

'You can come in. I found out what it was.'

She turned her face in the bed and looked at him.

'Gettin' lazy, aren't I?'

She gave a long deep sigh, as if against the heat and tiredness of the day, and spread out her plump bare arms across the bed. He stood looking at her for some moments, attracted and bewildered, tortured between the visual image of her lying there, of the dark-haired supine body relaxed as if waiting for him, and the hard and painfully difficult thought that now he must pay her what he owed.

Suddenly all his tortured thought seemed to resolve itself. He came forward another pace or two and began to make trembling and clumsy efforts to touch her.

'Here,' she said, 'this won't get the money paid –'

Once again he was human and tender.

'I want you,' he said. His hands were beginning to tremble violently. 'I want you – I can't git on without you –'

'You keep all on, don't you? Mind my dress.'

'Dulcie,' he said. 'God –'

'Mind my dress then. And don't call me Dulcie. My name's Dulcima.'

'Dulcima,' he said quietly. 'Dulcima.'

He ran his hands about her relaxed soft throat and shoulders, trembling, seeking with gestures of great clumsiness to express what he felt and what he wanted.

'Here, I thought you came to pay me the money,' she said.

'I did. So I did. I got it.'

'Put it on the wash-stand then,' she said. He seemed to hesitate. 'Go on –'

She lingered on the words and something about them seemed to inflame him, so that he moved almost blindly as he groped about, taking the money from his trousers' pocket. 'How much?' he said. 'How much?'

'Forty pounds,' she said. 'Just forty. Well, all but two shilling –'

For a moment he was shattered. He had moved across to the wash-stand like a man in a coma of heavy excitement and now, for a single moment, the notion of that extraordinary figure of forty pounds seemed to wake him up. He turned on her sharply. His mouth gaped open as if, in a flash of revelation, he had seen what a fool he was.

And then he stopped. He saw that she had taken off her dress and that now she was sitting up on the bed, casually and half undressed, rolling down her stockings. He heard her say something about 'put it in the drawer, it'll be out of the way there' and in blind excitement he stuffed what money he had into the drawer of the wash-stand.

When he groped back to her it was to be stricken by another troubling and this time more painful thought.

'What about Albert?' he said.

'You don't think I ever wanted Albert,' she said, 'do you?'

She looked past him with a long slow smile.

'Did Albert ever –?'

'Does it matter if he did?' she said.

Frenziedly he reached out for her and she smiled, letting him kiss her for the first time. She held her face sideways, so that the black close eyes were fixed on the evening sky. The evening was still warm and blue and beautiful and now she seemed to see something in it that split the dark pupils for another second with yet another smile.

5

SHE did not go to market on the following day. 'I'll glean a little corn for the hens,' she said. 'You enjoy yourself. You'll get on better without me.'

During the morning, when Parker had gone, she discovered, for the first time, what lay in the little attic above the steps and what, in turn, lay above that too.

Parker, the previous night, had left his working clothes in her bedroom. In the morning she had taken the key of the attic from his trousers and later he had gone away in the suit, with the black hat, he always wore for market.

When she went up into the little attic she was surprised to find it empty except for a shelf on which stood rows of biscuit tins. At first she did not bother to look into these tins. She went up another flight of steps on to the roof above. A square balustraded platform had been built there by some previous owner who had evidently wanted the air, the stars, the sun or simply the long view, across twenty miles of valley, to the sea.

She stood for some time fascinated by this view. It opened out a world that lay below her like a map. She could see not only the fields she knew, bare and white after the heat of summer and harvest, but small chalky veins of road winding away among clotted copses of sweet chestnut, through fox-red villas and fields of dark green potatoes. She could see, five or six miles away, the square stone church tower of the market town and then, far beyond it, delicate and faint, the line of sea horizon, with a few creeping charcoal puffs that were the smoke of passing steamers. It created for her the curious and heady illusion that here, above everything, alone and on top of the world, she had never been able to see so far.

After some minutes she went down into the attic. She smiled occasionally when she thought of Parker: Parker so clever, so tight, so mean and so eager; Parker so desperate for her, so childish and so like a man. She smiled when she thought of his rushing, clumsy affection and she smiled still more when she opened the first of the biscuit tins.

In them, in many neat tied bundles of notes, Parker kept his money. There were six biscuit tins and there were even empty biscuit tins waiting to be filled.

At first she did not touch the money. Instead she went back to her bedroom. She found the money Parker had given her and she counted it. There were fifteen pounds.

As she discovered it, she smiled another curious sideways smile and then went back to the attic. She opened one of the biscuit tins and took another twenty-five pounds; and then, as an afterthought, another ten. Then she closed the biscuit tins and went downstairs.

All that day she did as she had told Parker she would: she gleaned corn for the hens from the lower wheat field. It was very hot in the white chalk cup of land below the hill and she felt the sun burn her as she worked solidly up and down with heavy movements of her thick brown legs and arms. Work and the long hot summer had taken a little flesh from her, so that her limbs were harder and smoother, without the flabbiness of the days when she had pushed the pram up the hill. Her dark eyes were keener and brighter, more penetrating and more mature. She had found more time to brush her hair and gradually it had lost its coarseness. She even thought there were times when her legs were not so ugly as before.

Once during the afternoon she looked up and there, at the foot of the hill, by the gate, she saw once again the young man with the gun, the man that Barnes had seen. He seemed to hesitate for a moment as she looked up, and then he began to walk across the field towards her.

She went on gathering corn-straw until he came up to her. He was very much taller than she was, with a big frame and a shock of thick hair that pushed from under his cap.

'Beg pardon, Mrs Parker.'

'Who are you calling Mrs Parker?'

'Oh,' he said. In this awkward moment he could do nothing but look away from her, fidgeting with the stock of his gun. 'Well – I only wanted to say – I got young pheasants up in the wood there. Sometimes they get across here on your piece –'

'If they get on here they belong here,' she said.

'Yes, but –'

'He don't like people roaming about the land. Parker don't like it, pheasants or no pheasants.'

'I only want to walk across once in a while,' he said. 'Say once a day.'

'I think you better keep off,' she said. 'He don't like it.'

'Not if I asked him?'

'Wouldn't make no difference. He don't like folks traipsing round.'

'Would you ask him?'

'Me?'

'I'd be glad if you'd ask him,' he said, 'will you?'

'Well, I'll see,' she said. 'But for the lord's sake don't come on until I say. He's funny that way. He don't like people on here.'

'I see. Well, thanks,' he said and began to walk away.

Twenty yards away something seemed to occur to him and he turned and called back:

'If you want me any time I'm up in the wood. I got a hut there. You'll find me.'

When Parker came home about four o'clock he was less drunk than sleepy. 'Let me take your hat and coat,' she said. 'You have a nap in the chair.'

She took his hat and coat and laid them in the sitting-room. After a time she looked into the hat. Sixty-five pounds, all in notes, were folded into the brim, and she took out fifteen. She laid the fifteen pounds on the kitchen table and when Parker woke up and came to the table for tea she said:

'This is that money you give me last night. I did say fourteen, didn't I?'

'Yeh, yeh,' he said. He spoke with sleepy eagerness; he remembered how, the previous night, she had clearly spoken of forty and of how he had put only fifteen, in that tense excited moment of seeing her undressing, in the wash-stand drawer. 'Yeh, that was it, fourteen.'

'Well you give me too much. You give me fifteen.'

'I did?'

'You better have a pound back,' she said. 'We want things right, don't we?'

'No, no, go on,' he said. 'That's for you. You have it. You keep that.' He smiled and leaned across the table and ran his hand briefly about her neck. 'That's for you. That's for the little extras.'

She smiled too, sleepy and casual, and said, letting him caress her: 'You like the little extras, do you?'

He was fired with small frenzies of excitement and leaned farther over and kissed her face, brown and warm from sun. She laughed and suddenly it seemed to him marvellously good and clever and satisfying to have her there, to have got away with the small deceit of the fifteen pounds, and to hear her laughing because he touched her.

'You better get on with your tea,' she said. 'There's a time and place –'

He tried roughly to smother her mouth with kisses and she said:

'Go on with you. You'll knock your tea over and then you'll know about it.'

Then as he laughed and let her go, she said:

'About this money. It's quite a bit. I thought I'd bank it.'

'Banks? You don't want t'ave nothing to do with no banks,' he said. 'Banks ain't no good.'

'No?'

'They git to know too much. They know all your business. Then the income tax git to know. I ain't payin' no tax if I know it – they ain't gittin' nothing away from me.'

'I'll put it in the post office,' she said. 'I'll git interest.'

'You don't wanta do nothing with it,' he said. 'You

keep it. You keep it where nobody can't touch it. That's all.'

'Well, I'll see,' she said.

Suddenly, off-hand, casually, as if it were something of no great importance, she changed the subject.

'Oh! I forgot –' She was telling the truth now; there was no need to lie any longer when she could simply repeat the details of a straightforward circumstance – 'that fellow with the gun – he come prowling round again today.'

'Albert?'

'I don't know, I don't know,' she said. In sudden nervousness she spoke quickly. 'He was right across the field. He sheered off through the wood before I could tell.'

'I'll sheer him off,' he said. 'Damn quick. What's he want with you now?'

'I don't know, I can't think,' she said. 'Why don't he leave us alone. I told him. I told him about –'

'Told him?' he said. 'Told him about what?'

'About us,' she said. 'About how we were. You know – about being on our own up here and all that. The two of us.'

Parker, with thoughts buzzing in his head like crazy flies, trembled with joy. He suddenly exulted in the notion that he had cheated Albert. At first he had simply been jealous of Albert, but now he had cheated him. It was a clever deal to have cheated Albert. It was a wonderful thing to know that Albert had been rejected.

And now, because of it, he felt more sure of Dulcima. Once or twice he had not been quite so sure. Sometimes when she had spoken of Albert it evoked in him the small, sour, disturbing thought that she was not playing straight with him, that it was really always Albert she liked most, Albert she preferred.

But now he knew that that was not so. Things were different now. Albert was finished, and it was only himself she wanted.

6

Two days later she put her money in the post office bank. She rode down to the town by bus, coming back in the afternoon with the new clean post office book in her handbag, thinking how pleasant the first figure in it was; how solid and how satisfactory and how secret; and how, in time, if she were careful and things went well, she could make this figure grow.

The bus stopped on the corner below the hill. She had to walk the last mile to the farm. In two or three days it would be September. A few late fingers of honeysuckle, pale yellow, touched with flecks of strawberry, were still flowering on the high bank above the lane and she suddenly felt an impulse to climb the bank to gather them.

From there she could see across a copse of hazel that had been cut down in springtime. Beyond it great beeches, still green, faintly brown only when scorched by sun, rose for almost a mile along the steep hillside of chalk. And as she stood there, gathering the honeysuckle, smelling it, thinking a little, she saw the young keeper walking down the path.

He saw her at the same moment and began to come down beside the hazel copse, almost as if he had been waiting for her. She saw him coming and began to behave at once as if she had not seen him, going on gathering the honeysuckle, turning her back, slowly walking away down the hill.

'I got something I wanted to say,' he said.

'Oh?'

Slowly she picked off sprigs of honeysuckle, not looking at him.

'I been wanting to see you,' he said.

'Me? Why me?'

'I wanted to say I was sorry I called you Mrs Parker.'

She did not speak for a moment. She held her head sideways and put the honeysuckle to her nose and the curling flowers of it seemed to climb, tendrilwise and delicate, about her brown cheeks. It was like a small gesture of enticement that she had made unintentionally.

'I'm sorry I said that,' he said. 'I didn't know.'

'Didn't know what?'

'Well –'

'You don't want to get ideas in your head.'

'I only just come here,' he said. 'I don't know folks –'

'Still, you don't want to get ideas,' she said. 'I don't like people getting ideas.'

He stood awkwardly, not knowing what to say. The hedge, with its pale yellow curling fingers of honeysuckle, stood between them like a barrier. Something made her run her fingers through the topmost leaves of it as she turned and moved along it and then he called:

'There was something else. Did you ask him?'

'Ask him what?'

'About the pheasants – about walking over –'

'I told you it's more than my life's worth,' she said. 'He flies into a two-and-eight now if anybody so much as looks at the land.'

46

'Shall I ask him?' he said.

'You want to get your brains blown out?' she said.

She held the honeysuckle to her face again and once more, fine and tendrilwise, the flowers delicately fingered the skin of her summer-brown face and once more she responded by walking away.

'The honeysuckle's nice,' he said.

'Yes. It smells nice. I like the smell.'

'There's been a fine lot farther along the wood,' he said, 'on top of the hill.'

'Really?'

'It's nice up there,' he said. 'Nobody ever goes much up there.'

Later, as she walked away across the hill, she was aware of him standing there, still watching her. She was aware also of wanting to look back. She did not look back and she began to feel vaguely uneasy about something without knowing what it was. A light prickling of sunlight came down through the beech-leaves and made a pattern of light and shadow on her face. Unconsciously she let the honeysuckle finger her mouth again, and it made her look more thoughtful than ever.

Some evenings later, when she sat at supper with Parker, she began to cry.

'Here,' said Parker. 'Here. What now?'

'I can't find the money,' she said. 'That money you give me.'

'Musta mislaid it somewheres, that's all.'

'I looked high and low,' she said.

'When'd you see it last?'

'That day I was gleaning,' she said. 'That day Albert

was prowling around. I went out and never locked the house.'

'Gawd,' said Parker. 'We gotta stop this.'

'Don't do nothing yet,' she said. 'We don't want no trouble.'

She cried again as Parker looked about him with small uneasy rabbity eyes.

'Don't cry,' he said. 'That won't do no good.'

'Yes, but I got nothing now. What have I got? I paid all that out – them curtains and all that – and now it's gone –'

'I'll make it up to you. I'll make it right,' Parker said.

After some time she stopped crying.

'I made a mistake that first time,' she said. 'I added it up wrong. You put me off that night, coming into the bedroom. Its twenty-four pounds ten to be right. I forgot two stewpans and I never put the curtain-tapes down.'

Parker looked troubled and reflective. Several months had gone by since that first evening she had washed his face and talked of new curtains; and it was hard now, almost impossible, to work out how much he might have owed.

'It's only a bit extra,' she said. 'It's not much.' Now she in turn took his head in her hands and smoothed his face. 'You can't have all the little extras for nothing, can you?'

For some days Parker was troubled about the money. He began to make furtive and inconclusive searches among the biscuit tins. He had never been quite sure, to within forty or fifty or even a hundred pounds, how much they held; sometimes when he came home from market, over-drunk, jubilant at the thought of fifty or sixty pounds folded into his hat, he had woken up to find himself on the kitchen floor, some part of his memory paralysed, so that he could not remember exactly how much the hat had held.

At the same time his thoughts of Dulcima deepened. He thought of how good she was, how capable, how hard-working; how she had got her head screwed on the right way. He thought much more of her brown, smooth, hardening body; he thought of her as she was in the bedroom. He felt that if he married Dulcima he could take her into his confidence. He would be able to tell her about the money upstairs. He had the impression that she was a shrewd careful girl who perhaps could help him, in time, to make more money. That was the sort of partner he wanted.

Then again, he would think, it was cheaper to marry. Three pounds a week: that was a lot of money for a girl, too much money. The two of them could live for that. They could, he thought, enjoy all that they were enjoying now but enjoy it more often and enjoy it cheaper. Marriage was the thing; marriage was the answer.

Then he remembered too that she had once been going to marry Albert and his jealousy about Albert began to be renewed. It was odd how Albert was always cropping up. He remembered the incident of Albert in the wheatfield, staring over the gate with his gun, Albert at the Market, Albert prowling round, Albert having to be told about things, Albert always after her. He remembered how once the notion of Albert doing these things had seemed funny and how he thought he had cheated him.

But now it was not funny; he was not so sure. He began to want Dulcima for himself. More and more he wanted to be sure of her and to be rid of Albert for ever.

So he spoke of getting married. 'Eh? How about that?' he said. 'You know how folks are – start talkin'. We could git married at one o' them offices any day. Eh?'

'I got to think it over.'

'All right, you think it over.'

And as the days passed she would think it over; or rather she would pretend to think it over. She would think instead of her bank-book, the money in the biscuit tins, and the way the money could grow; she would smile at the thought of Parker and his little extras and how, for some time longer, she would keep him waiting for an answer.

Then as the days grew shorter, Parker began to think of long winter nights, with western winds howling wet sea-storms against the hill. He thought of snow. Sometimes snow lay so long and deep in the narrow hill-lanes that he could not get out for a month to the market. He felt he did not want to face the snow, the storms, the darkness, and the rain alone again in another winter. He dreaded a cold empty bed and the dark crust of winter settling over everything as it had done last year, before Dulcima had arrived to sweep it away.

'Well, Dulcima, you made up your mind –?'

'Oh! I don't know. I want to – it ain't that, but there's a lot o' things –'

'It ain't Albert, is it?'

'Albert – good Lord, no.'

'What is it then?'

'Well, once you're married, you're married. I don't want to jump out of the frying pan into the fire,' she said, laughing, 'do I?'

'When are you going to make up your mind? Soon, eh? Afore winter.'

'Some day.'

She noticed how her little trick of mocking him started fires of excitement in his eyes. 'Course you might have to marry me, yet. You know that, don't you?'

'That wouldn't worry me,' he said.

'I should think not,' she said. 'I'm the one to worry about a thing like that.'

'You think it over then – quick,' he said. 'Think it over – afore winter comes.'

But as she lay awake at night, on the soft windless darkness of early October, she did not think it over. She thought of other things. She thought mostly, at first, of the money, the biscuit tins, the bank-book and the simple way she had been able to arrange these things. She thought of how easily, after all, she had been able to get the things she had never had. She remembered her father, the barrier standing between herself and a new dress or new shoes or new white gloves or a little freedom or a little money. She remembered the children coming one after another, and then the days with the pram, all of them frustrating her. Now she was finished with them all: the children, her father, the pram, the days of tugging and standing and pushing until her legs were gross and hideous, and she was glad that they were over.

She thought also of the young man standing by the hedge of honeysuckle, watching her as she walked away through the wood of beeches. She remembered the curious sensation that seemed to impel her to turn round and look back at him. In the warm October darkness it was a sensation that somehow began to magnify itself. It grew not only larger but more mystifying. It fascinated and haunted her, so that she lay awake for a long time with her eyes stiffened with sleeplessness, staring at the stars above the hill, wondering why it fascinated her and why it roamed tirelessly and hauntingly round and round in her mind.

Then, at last, it began to trouble her.

7

ONE afternoon in late October she walked through the beech-wood, above the farm, to the keeper's hut on the far slope of the hill. The leaves of the beeches were already making masses of fire against a sky that was blue and lofty and under them the glow of air was a pure orange, full of dancing flies.

The door of the keepers' hut was open but the hut was empty and her feeling of disappointment was so sharp that it took her by surprise. She had not expected that. Inside the hut there was a table, a camp-bed, two chairs, an oilstove and a few cups and a box below the bed. A row of oiled steel traps hung on one wall and a neat pile of newspapers lay on the table, with a pair of leather gloves and a canvas bag.

She felt a curious uneasy sensation of excitement as she looked at these things. There was a neatness, a swept homeliness about the hut that fascinated her. A bucket with a galvanized lip for soap stood in one corner with a towel folded over the side. A mirror by the window above it had a hairbrush and comb hanging on one side and a razor-strop on the other.

For winter there was a stove and for some reason she thought suddenly of winter rain, of days of flying beech-leaves, of the little hut with the stove humming away behind the closed door. There was something wonderfully secure in thinking about these things, and that too took her by surprise.

She walked away up the hill. At the crest of it a breeze came over the bare western slope where the copses of hazel had been cut down. It blew her hair about her face and down over her cheeks in untidy strands. The honey-suckle the young man had spoken about had dropped its flowers and now hung with reddening berries over bushes of hawthorn.

She walked back down the hill. Half-way to the hut the sound of a gun-shot came from the far side of the wood, rushing like a rocket through the fiery ceiling of leaves. She went on and stood for some moments at the door of the hut. This time she noticed on the wall inside a pattern of blown birds' eggs, some hundreds of them, blue and white and scribbled and spotted and brown, strung together in necklaces, the eggs graded like beads. They too fascinated her. They too had that wonderful neatness and secureness about them that left her uneasy and surprised.

As she went inside the hut to look more closely at the pattern of eggs making ten-fold necklaces on the dark wall, she caught sight of her face with its untidy strands of blown hair in the mirror by the window.

She stood by the mirror and began to comb back her hair with her fingers. Her hair had always tended to grow in heavy side-fingers that had the effect of thickening her face. It grew low over her forehead and was greasy. Suddenly she picked up the comb and began to comb the wind-blown strands of hair back from her forehead and her ears. The sensation of the comb scraping over the crest of her forehead and through her matted hair was so minutely painful for a moment that she bit her lips. She was angry with herself and suddenly hated the face she saw in the mirror, with the too thick, too dark, too greasy hair. It brought back for a moment a memory of her father. She felt a stab of her old grievance about being beautiful. She remembered how much she wanted to have a different body: a different kind of face, different eyes, different hands, above all different legs and hair.

'Who would look at a face like that?' she thought.

She was savagely brushing her hair when she heard the young man set his gun down by the door of the hut. She was so startled that she had no time to put down the brush. She felt the blood rushing to her face and then an embarrassing trembling of her hands.

'It's all right. Make yourself at home,' he said. 'I saw you coming down.'

'You saw me?'

'Not many people I miss,' he said. 'That's what I'm here for.'

'I didn't think you saw me –'

She did not know what to do with the brush in her hands.

'I'm using your brush – the wind got into my hair. I can never do anything with it. I don't know what you'll think of me –'

'That's all right,' he said.

'I really come in to look at your birds' eggs. The door was open and I could see them and I come in.'

'That's all right.'

The blood was pounding up through her neck and face

and into the roots of her hair, and she was gripping the brush with both hands.

'I'm sorry – it's not very nice coming in like that and using other people's brushes and all that – but I never thought –'

'I'm going to make some tea,' he said. 'What about a cup o' tea?'

'I think I ought to go,' she said. 'I think I made a nuisance of myself enough for one day.'

'That's all right. Stay and have a cup o' tea.'

She watched him, still with the brush in her hands, put a match to a little oil stove on a stand by the window. She saw him fill an enamel kettle from a bucket underneath it. He put two mugs on the table, with a tin of sugar and a bottle of milk, and a teapot and two spoons. She was fascinated again by the neatness of everything, the order, the completeness of his private world.

'You always live here?' she said.

'March to November.'

'You sleep here?'

'Everything,' he said.

He turned to find a chair for her and she saw his eyes shine pale blue, almost white, in the brilliance of low October light by the doorway.

'Don't you find it lonely?'

'Me? No: I like it.'

'I think I should find it lonely.'

'Depends what you're used to,' he said.

It was only when she turned to sit down at last that she became aware again of the brush. She was still trembling as she laid it on the little shelf under the mirror.

'I don't know what you think of me – with your brush and all that –'

But he was pouring water into the teapot, with his back to her, and did not answer.

In her nervousness, as she sat at the table with him, drinking tea, she could think of nothing to talk about but the long necklaces of blown eggs hanging behind him on the wall. The semi-circles of blue and brown and white framed his face each time she turned to look at him.

'Them?' he said. 'That's my score. Three hundred and twenty since March.'

'That keeps you busy. That's why you're not lonely,' she said.

'Found a magpie's only last week,' he said. 'It's one I missed somehow: one egg.'

'That was one for sorrow,' she said. 'Or is it joy? I can never remember.'

'I don't know. They're all magpies to me. All vermin. I can't bother about sorrow or joy.'

And then: 'Talking about my score, I think the brush makes us even. You know – for when I called you Mrs Parker.'

'Oh! that.'

All of a sudden she was astonished by a wave of repugnance about Parker. It rushed up into her head to chill the last of the hot blood of her embarrassment about the brush.

'I didn't think,' he said. 'You know – it was natural.'

'I just housekeep for him,' she said. 'He got nobody to

57

look after him after his wife died. I felt sorry for him. I just did it to oblige. That's all – I shan't stay long.'

'No?'

'No. I don't want to stay there all my life, do I?'

For some moments he did not speak again. He held the mug of tea just under his face, in both hands, his elbows on the table, his lips blowing slightly. On his top lip the hairs were long and soft and remarkably golden as if the sun bleached them as they grew freshly every day.

'Do you sleep there?' he said.

'Who me?' she said. 'Not likely. I go back home every night.'

As she lied she felt a rush of new embarrassment spring up and meet, in a sickening impact, the cold wave of a new repugnance about Parker.

'Here, I hope you don't get ideas,' she said. 'I hope you don't think –'

'No,' he said. 'No. I didn't mean –'

'I should hope not. I should think so,' she said. 'It's bad enough having to be stuck up here, all alone half the time. Half the time nobody to talk to. Nobody to see –'

'Well, now you can come and see me,' he said.

She felt at that moment a wave of quite different feeling gather and slowly proceed, without violence, up through her body. It had the effect of softening, then dispelling the last of her embarrassment and she said:

'Is that asking me? Is it an invitation?'

'I like somebody to talk to –'

'Is it an invitation?'

'Yes,' he said.

The remarkable flow of new warm feeling spread at last over all her body, making her smile.

'Will you come?'

'Yes,' she said. 'I'd like to.'

Later, as she walked down the path through the wood, away from the hut, she had again the curious feeling that he was watching her from behind. She was harassed by an overwhelming instinct that she must turn and look at him. This time she did turn, and then when she turned he was not there. Only clouds of golden October flies were dancing by the hut in the sunshine.

That night she lay awake for longer than usual. She thought of the incredible private neatness of the hut: the skeins of birds' eggs, the singing of the kettle on the stove, the smell of tea and oil and spent cartridges, the way she had brushed her hair. She remembered his question about where she slept at nights and what she had said in answer.

'I done wrong about that,' she thought. 'I never ought to have said that.' She felt a sudden complication of thought that was too much for her. She stared sleeplessly, in remorse, at the October stars.

'Now I don't know where I am,' she thought. 'I don't know where I am.'

8

As October went on she began to walk up into the wood almost every afternoon. 'I'll see for a few blackberries,' she would say to Parker, 'else a few nuts.' Or she would suddenly get her black leather shopping bag and say, as if on the spur of the moment: 'I just remembered I got no baking powder in the house. I'll walk down as far as the shop. Is there anything you want? I'll bring it if you do.'

Sometimes the door of the hut was open and the hut itself empty. She would stand outside under the gleaming orange October beeches or sit inside at the neat swept table, waiting for a while. She would find herself fascinated again by the neatness of everything, the seclusion, the clean and solid privacy. She would feel herself grow excited by the smell of oil in traps, of tea, of spent cartridges and dying leaves. Then she would suddenly feel sick about Parker. Her repugnance about him would begin to drive her like an ugly rat. She would feel, again, that she did not know where she was. She was lost somewhere between the haunting repugnance about Parker and the haunting nervousness about the keeper, whose name she did not know. And suddenly she would turn and hurry back down the hill, through flying shoals of beech-leaves, frightened of herself, back to Parker and the farm.

On another day the young man would be sitting in the

hut, alone and quiet, exactly as she pictured him and exactly as she wanted him to be. She would sit for a time talking, listening to the quiet flame of the stove. He would make tea and she would watch, in stillness, but without assurance or confidence, the movement of his large bony hands.

Then she would try, with hesitation, awkwardly, to find what lay behind the calmness, the assured quietness, the half-averted, pale, transparent eyes.

Didn't he ever go down to market? To the pictures once in a while?

'No,' he said. 'By the time I'm finished and cleaned up here I'm about ready for bed.'

Didn't he feel he wanted an evening out some time? Didn't he feel he'd go off his head up there, alone in the wood, same thing day after day, without a bit of a change?

'I sometimes get down as far as the main road on Sundays,' he said. 'Walk down and watch the cars.'

'You do?' she said. 'I go that way sometimes. Do you know *The Rose of Tralee*? That's down there. On the corner. It's a café.'

'No,' he said. 'I just walk round.'

'They have tea,' she said, 'and ice-cream and all that. You can have it in the garden. They have tables in the garden.'

'That's nice,' he said.

'They wanted me to work there once,' she said. 'In the kitchen. They offered me a good job there once. I sometimes think I should have took it. I sometimes think I ought to go down and ask them if they still wanted anybody. What do you think?'

'You should go down,' he said.

'Yes,' she said, 'I think I'll walk down on Sunday. What time do you go down?'

'Most Sundays I got to be here,' he said. 'If I got a big shoot on Monday I got to get ready for that.'

She noticed he spoke with half-averted eyes, as if he were a long way away from her: as if, she thought, he could not bear to come nearer or even look at her.

One afternoon she did not walk up to the wood. She took the bus and her big black shopping bag and went into town. She had begun to experience a sudden hunger for new shoes. She felt the need for a pair of gloves for her hands. She was troubled once again by the ugliness of her feet and hands and legs, the clumsy shortness of her body. She spent some time in shoe shops, buying herself finally a pair of black patent shoes with oval buckles and then a lighter pair, pale grey, with higher heels, in suede. She had never before had money for shoes like that and suddenly she felt driven by a new excitement.

'And stockings? Would you want stockings?' the assistant said. 'We keep stockings.'

As Dulcima fingered the silk stockings with her coarse and stumpy hands she recalled, once again with hatred, the ugliness of her thick legs and ankles. She bought three pairs of stockings and then 'I gotta get a dress too,' she thought. 'No sense having new shoes and stockings and not a dress.'

For the rest of the afternoon, as she went from shop to shop, it was as if she peeled off old skins of her life: shoes, cotton stockings kept up with black garters, straight print dress bleached by sun and washing, old underwear having broken straps fixed up with safety pins. As she tried on dresses in fitting cubicles she was more and more painfully aware of the shabbiness, the sloppy shapelessness of herself. The dresses seemed like stretched sacks on her big breasts and waist and thighs. 'It's not that you're bad for size,' assistants told her. 'But you need support. You would find it better with support.' She had never bothered with corsets and sometimes, alone up at the farm, in hot weather, with only Parker to see her, not even with a brassière. Now she bought them. She saw herself as she had seen so many advertisements of women, over and over again, in newspapers and magazines: her breasts cupped and held upright, her short thick back and thighs curved in oyster, the stretched front of herself gleaming silkily.

She bought a pair of white kid gloves and she thought finally of a hat. It took her some time to decide against a hat. She decided on a perm for her hair instead. 'You will have to make an appointment,' they told her and she said:

'It has to be before Sunday. I got to have it before Sunday.'

'We can manage Friday,' they said. 'At three in the afternoon.'

When she got back to the farm after going to the hair-dresser on Friday afternoon Parker had not come home from market. She went upstairs and sat in her bedroom and stared at herself in the glass. She saw her face as she might have seen the face of another person. She felt it was strange and unreal and beautiful. 'You're rather on the short side,' the hairdresser had said, 'so I'm going to build it up a bit to give you height.' Her hair was mounted now in a series of stiff black lustreless waves that, rising to a crown, made her face seem longer and less podgy. The untidy strands that had covered her ears and the sides of her cheeks had been cut away. She was able to see, almost as it might have been for the first time, the shape of her ears. Free of hair, they were surprisingly long and shapely and they too, she thought, had the effect of uplifting her.

For some moments she ran a comb through her hair very gently, hardly daring to touch it. 'Comb it our carefully,' the hairdresser had said. 'It will look better when you have combed it and it has settled down.'

Then she remembered the young man in the wood and suddenly she had an overpowering desire to go up to the keeper's hut and discover what he felt about the strange and lovely change in herself. She did not think he could fail to see, as she did, a transformation.

'I never thought I could look like that,' she thought.

Then she wondered about her clothes. If the change in her hair could do so much for her what about the change in her clothes? She considered for a moment the idea of putting them on and then she thought:

'No. Sunday'll do. I'll wait till Sunday. I'll have a good strip-wash and be clean for Sunday.'

Then suddenly the overpowering desire to show herself to the young keeper came back. She wanted to share the sight of herself, so much changed, with another person.

She gave a final touch or two to her hair with the comb and then went downstairs. It took only a few minutes to go up to the wood, but she wanted to run with excitement. The smell of her hair was something new in her experience too and she wondered if he would notice its strong sweetness. It seemed to her to have a smell that was wonderfully dusky, a deep clove, like the smell of carnations.

In the kitchen Parker was slowly counting money, note by note, out of the greasy rim of his hat. She stopped abruptly. She had forgotten Parker. She was embarrassed and repelled by the sudden realization of Parker. She was sickened by the sight of the greasy hands pawing, with measured greed, into the greasy recesses of the hat.

'Eh, that you, Dulcima? I wondered where you was.'

The bleary eyes of Parker seemed to be pencilled, at the edges, with lines of sharp raw pink. He squinted at her as if he could not see her properly.

A few notes fell out of his unsteady hands into the bowl of his hat and he did not pick them up again. He seemed to grope, with moist, pink-lidded eyes, to focus a better impression of her.

'Dulcie – eh, Dulcie – what you done to yourself? What you bin doing to yourself?' he said.

'I had my hair done, that's all,' she said.

He groped for a moment or two longer in bleary astonishment, trying to correct the focus of the incredible image of her and the unfamiliar mass of piled curled hair.

66

She did not move. He seemed to be trying to convince himself that what he saw was not a drunk's illusion. He got up and began to come towards her with open hands, the pink-lidded eyes protuberant and inflamed.

'What made you do that?' he said. 'Makes you look different – I like it, it makes you look different. It looks nice. I like it – what made you have it done?'

'I had it done with that money you give me,' she said.

The excited notion flew down through his stupefied brain that, since she had done it with the money he had given her, she had also done it for himself.

'Dulcie, Dulcie,' he said. He began to grope for her neck and shoulders with excited, trembling hands. His nostrils gave a quivering upward start as he caught the extraordinary dusky smell of her hair. 'Dulcie, Dulcie,' he said, 'you thought any more about what I said – you know, about us, about what I said –?'

'No,' she said. 'No. Not yet – I want to wait a bit – I want to wait.'

She stood rigid while he began to pour wet kisses on her neck and cheeks and soft exposed ears.

'I can't wait much longer,' he said. 'Dulcie, I can't wait much longer –'

'I want to wait,' she said.

'Wait what for?' he said. 'What for? You know me, don't you? You bin here all summer – you know the place, don't you? You know what I got. I got plenty – I got more'n I know what to do with, Dulcie. I bin fly – I got plenty –'

'I want to wait,' she said.

He staggered about the table, reaching for his hat,

picking up notes, laughing as he tried to give her the money.

'I got plenty – you only got to say –'

'I don't want it. I want to wait,' she said.

'Here,' he said. 'Here –'

He suddenly seized her by the shoulders, laughing again, dragging her out of the room and upstairs. She let herself be drawn rigidly, without a word. 'You come with me, Dulcie – you come with me. I got summat to show you –' Trying to find his keys, he stumbled, fell on all fours and crawled the last few steps to the attic door on hands and knees.

'There y'are, Dulcie,' he said. 'What about that, eh? You never seen nothing like that afore.'

She stood in the attic staring at the rows of biscuit tins. She had no surprise about them and her hands were stiff by her sides.

'That's money for you, ain't it?' he said.

'I don't want it,' she said.

She found herself staring out of the window, her mind wandering, all her vision expanding out of the narrowness of the little room, out of the world of Parker, the money and the biscuit tins, to the valley lying below in the late October sunshine. In the sharp autumn air its distances seemed to be heightened and enlarged, taking her farther away than ever.

'There y'are,' Parker said. In a stupefied ecstasy of secret-sharing he fingered the money with one hand and then herself, in clumsy excitement, with the other. 'You don't want no more'n that, do you?'

She stared out of the window into a world whose distances seemed not only amazingly enlarged. They seemed to be pulsating, out as far as the quivering edges of horizon, bluish-copper from approaching sunset, with the deep discharge of her own emotions. She thought of the things she had bought herself: the shoes, the silk stockings, the underwear, the tight sleek corsets, the dress, and even, at last, the pair of white gloves that would hide her big coarse hands. She wanted suddenly to find them all and rush out with them, away from the ugly rat of her repugnance about Parker, and never come back.

'I want to wait,' she said.

'All right, you wait,' Parker said. 'Here – take a pound or two now. Buy yourself something nice.' He began to thrust notes into her hands and then, when her hands were too rigid to take them, into the neck of her dress. 'You take 'em – buy something – just for yourself.'

She was hardly aware of what he did to her.

'How long d'ye want to wait?' he said.

'Not long now,' she said. 'Not long.'

9

SHE lay awake for a long time in the night, thinking again of the clothes she had bought, coming slowly to a decision. She felt she could not wait even another day before she wore them for the first time. She came to a decision, too, about another thing.

'I got to go. I got to get out,' she thought. 'I don't know where I'll end up. I don't know where I am.'

Parker had a small orchard of late apples at the lower end of the farm and after dinner he took a horse and trolley and a long picking ladder and went down to gather them. He said what a nice day it was and how nice it would be if she came down, later, to give him a hand, and she saw him look with uneasy fondness at her hair.

'I'll see how I get on,' she said. 'I got to run down to the shop.'

For some minutes she watched the truck bump down the stony track that led beyond the oast-houses and the bullock-yard to the field and the orchard beyond. Then she found herself wondering what it would be like to be seeing him for the last time, and the thought exulted her. She found herself trembling as she went upstairs. She took a jug of hot water with her and in her bedroom she stripped herself and began to wash her face and body. She could still smell the dusky, clove-deep odour of her hair, fading a little now but still strong, and she longed for it to remain like that for at least that afternoon.

When she got into the new corset she stood for some time staring at herself in the glass. Then she put on her stockings and she stood up and stared at them too. It was the corset and the stockings, she thought, so sheer and smooth and shining, that did so much to alter all the tone and appearance of her body. The big bulges of her hips and stomach were carved down and held in a shell, and the veins of her legs, always like stiff blue worms, were hidden away. There was a division, too, between her breasts, instead of the sagging blown pillow that had always been there.

She was ready by three o'clock. As she went out of her bedroom she felt a sudden urge to make quite sure where Parker was. She climbed the stairs to the little balcony on the roof and looked down across the fields. She could see the tip of the ladder pointing up through the old red trees of apple and on the top of it the squat grey head of Parker, under the greasy hat, staring emptily like an owl. And once again she felt that she might be seeing him, that day, for the last time, and again the thought exulted her.

She walked up through the wood very slowly. Her body felt stiff in the unaccustomed corsets. She did not know quite what to do with her hands in the new white gloves and the heels of her shoes seemed to make her taller than she had expected.

It seemed like a strange accident when she saw the young keeper coming down the path to meet her. She felt nervous at the sight of him. The afternoon sun, low under masses of smouldering beeches, was dazzling in his eyes. She saw the blue fierce sparkle of them under ruckled brows.

He seemed suddenly unable to believe in the reality of her as she came up the path. He stopped and held his head sideways and squinted. Then he walked slowly towards her, imprisoned for a few moments longer in disbelief about herself, her new clothes, her new identity.

'It is you,' he said. 'I couldn't believe it. It is you.'

She felt herself trembling violently and could only say: 'It's my day off. You never saw me on my day off before.'

'I thought it was some stranger. I thought your day was Sunday.'

'It used to be,' she said. 'But now –' She hesitated as if she did not know quite how to frame what she had to say. She had lied so readily in the past that now it was not easy to tell the truth in a simple way.

'Will you walk part of the way with me?' she said.

'Which way?'

'I want to walk down to the village – I got to go down there for something –'

'I'll walk part of the way,' he said. 'I'd like to. You want to go by the bottom path? – it's nice in the sun.'

They walked for some distance on the dry chalk path, carved white into the hillside at the edge of the beeches, before she spoke again.

'I'm glad I saw you. I got something to tell you,' she said.

She looked down at her new black shoes. The toes of them were already dusty with the dry chalk of the path.

'That wasn't quite right what I said. It wasn't exactly right about my day off. That wasn't quite right.'

'No?'

'No,' she said.

'Is that what you wanted to tell me?'

'No,' she said. 'I wanted to tell you I was leaving there.'

He stopped on the path. His hands jerked across the front of his body as if for a moment he wanted to take hold of her.

'Is that true?' he said.

'Yes, it's true,' she said. Now when she told the truth she desired passionately to be believed. 'Why? – don't you believe me? Don't you believe it's true?'

'Yes,' he said. 'Only I wanted to be sure – I been waiting to hear you say that for a long time.'

Suddenly she knew that there was a change in him; she felt that they were drawing closer together. She did not speak for a long time as they walked along the path. She could only look down at her new shoes and see them growing cloudier every moment with the dust she raised from the chalk, and it was the shoes that made her speak at last.

'Look at my shoes – whatever do they look like? They look like nothing on earth.'

'I can dust them,' he said.

He began to take out his handkerchief.

'Not now. They'll be as bad again if you do,' she said. 'You could do them at the gate, couldn't you? Before I go down the road?'

'Are you coming back today?' he said.

'Yes.'

'How long before you come back?'

'I don't know,' she said. 'About hour. About that. I just got to go somewhere – I got to go down to see after that job I told you about. The one in the café.'

'Can I wait and take you back?'

'If you want to,' she said. 'Do you want to?'

They had reached the gate at the end of the path and in answer he pulled out his handkerchief and began to dust her shoes. She felt the touch of the handkerchief as it flicked against the silk of her stockings. She could feel his nervousness in the quick, too delicate movements of his hands, the nervousness exaggerating her own until suddenly she felt slightly giddy and put her hands on his shoulders.

For a few moments this first touch of him made her blind with excitement. She felt the beeches tremble about her like great orange breakers in the act of plunging downhill towards the sun.

When she could see clearly again she saw that he was standing upright. He was putting his handkerchief away in his pocket and speaking of how long she would be and how he hoped she would get the job and how he would meet her when she came back.

'Where will you meet me?' she said.

'Here,' he said. 'I'll watch for you coming up the road.'

She walked down to the café and ordered tea and sat drinking it slowly. She felt the flush of it heating her body, pounding through her blood and drugging her mind until there was no coherence in her thought. She felt mystified and wondering and slightly frightened of the change in her feelings exactly as she had been filled with wonder at the change in her body when she had first seen it, in its silky shell of corsets and stockings, in the glass.

When her thoughts at last began to come back to her, as she walked up the hill, they were very simple. In the night she would pack her things. In the morning she would be honest with Parker. In the afternoon she could go. In that simple way, she thought, there would be the end of Parker.

'I know where I am now,' she thought. 'I got to go while I can.'

She wanted to run the last hundred yards up the hill to where the young keeper was waiting under the long smouldering arch of beeches. Instead she plodded heavily forward, her big legs striking back to gain their power from the slope of the hill exactly as they had done in the days when she pushed the pram.

'Well here you are,' she said. 'Did you think I was never coming? Did you get tired of waiting?'

'Did you get the job?' he said.

'I got to go back another day.'

They walked for some distance along the path without speaking. Chalk dust rose again in small white puffs and gradually sprinkled its bloom on her shoes. He looked once or twice at her shoes before saying nervously at last:

'They're getting whiter and whiter. Shall I dust them?'

'In a minute,' she said. 'I'll find somewhere to sit down in a minute. It'll be easier like that.'

They were three or four hundred yards from the farm

when she sat down on a beech-stump and put her feet and legs together so that he could dust her shoes. In the strong flat sunshine she was dazzled and could see nothing of the valley beyond his head. Half blind again, she was aware only of the movements, for the second time too quick and too delicate, of his hands about her shoes and ankles.

A moment later he was touching her legs. He was trying to say with coherence that he thought how beautiful she looked in the new shoes and the new stockings, but the words were too clumsy and too eager and suddenly the incredible stumbling fact of someone touching her legs and finding them beautiful was too much for her.

She got up and stood against him. As he held her she felt the entire front of her body turn molten and quivering. She shut her eyes against the strong gold glare of the sun and felt suddenly an extraordinary sensation of nakedness as she stood there on the open path and let him kiss her for the first time.

'I don't know what it is,' he said, 'but you're all different today. You look all different. Somehow it don't seem like you –'

'It's me all right,' she said. 'It's only the things I got on – the new things.'

She put her big awkward mouth up to him again, standing on the toes of her new shoes so that she could reach his face.

'Be here tomorrow,' she said. 'I got my things to bring. You'll be here, won't you?'

'What time?'

'Two o'clock.' She again had the queer uneasy sensation of nakedness, a strange impression of standing there starkly for the whole valley to see.

'Come into the wood,' she said. 'It's better out of the sun.'

In the shadow of the wood, under the coppery diffusion of light filtering down through crowds of turning leaves, she held his face in her new white gloves. Under their whiteness the skin of his face seemed a darker bronze than ever. He looked down at her with eyes transfixed in a deep and fond transparence, running his hands backwards and forwards over her head, and she wondered if he could smell the strong clove fragrance of her hair.

'How am I different?' she said.

'I don't know,' he said. 'Just different. I don't know how it is.'

She remembered how long she had wanted to be different and her wonder at being a new person in the eyes of someone else became, for the moment, almost too much for her to bear. In her happiness she felt her eyes slowly filling with tears.

'Come and meet me tomorrow,' she said. 'You will, won't you? Come down to meet me – because tomorrow I'm coming for good.'

10

THAT afternoon she did not know at first, though she knew it afterwards, that Parker stood watching her as she came down the hillside from the wood in the strong flame of sunlight to the farm. For a few moments, as she walked into the kitchen, still dazzled by what had happened and by the fierce brightness across the hill, she did not even remember that he existed. She stood slowly taking off her gloves, pulling at the white fingers one by one, staring and dazed and not seeing the kitchen about her.

The sound of Parker's voice was like the grating of a rusty hinge.

'Where you bin? Where you bin gone all afternoon?'

'I been out – I had to go out somewhere,' she said.

Slowly the squinting rabbity-eyes enlarged, grey and then stark white in their distension, under the powerful disbelief of what he saw. She saw his mouth quiver in a jibber of astonishment as he stood by the table and stared. Like the young man he seemed unable to recognize in her the person he had known.

'What you done to yourself?' he said. 'Dulcie – what you done?'

In disbelief, touched by wonder, he started to come towards her. He moved in a groping sort of fashion, his hands slightly outstretched.

'Dulcie – it don't look like you – where'd you get them things?'

For a second or two she felt afraid of him. She was locked in fear by the enlarging, colourless, possessive eyes. Then, in her fear, before she was aware of it and before she could stop it, she said the natural thing:

'You give me the money for them – don't you remember? You give me the money –'

His sudden joy at remembering this simple fact made his eyes contract. They closed with a paroxysm of delight. When they opened again they seemed to flare warmly, almost with laughter.

'Gawd, so I did – I did, didn't I? I give y'it, that's right –'

'I better go upstairs and take 'em off,' she said. 'I got your tea to get. I don't want to get 'em mucky.'

'No,' he said, 'don't go. Keep 'em on – it's Saturday night. You keep 'em on. We'll go out somewhere –'

'I don't want to go out nowhere,' she said. 'I got work to do. I got things to do –'

He came close to her, putting his hands on her bare thick brown arms. His excitement, swollen by disbelief, seemed to suck greedily at recollection.

'Dulcie, I ain't seen you lately – you know, we ain't – You know what I mean – you know, like we used to.'

'I got to take my things off,' she said. 'I got to go upstairs afore I get 'em spoiled.'

'I won't spoil 'em,' he said. 'I got a right to see 'em haven't I? You got 'em for me, didn't you?'

'No!' she said. The word seemed to shriek itself, ejected by a pure shot of fear, before she could prevent it.

'No?' he said. 'You never?'

This time the sudden enlargement of his eyes was frenzied. They shone with glassy fury, swollen grossly.

'No?' he shouted. 'Then who the 'ell did you get 'em for?'

'Nobody. Nobody.'

'You got yourself up for somebody! Who was it?'

'Nobody. Nobody,' she said.

She started to back away from him. The one glove she had taken off had dropped on to the kitchen table and now she remembered and tried to grab it as she moved. It fell from the table and she stooped anxiously to pick it up. She became aware at the same moment of his hand swinging savagely in air, but whether to hit her or grab her or pick up the glove she never knew. She ducked and ran.

As she ran upstairs she heard the incredible stupefying shout:

'It's Albert, ain't it? I know – it's Albert – it's Albert, ain't it?'

She had forgotten Albert. She was so much at a loss to know what he meant by Albert that she stumbled against the stairs, grabbing the old-fashioned banisters to prevent herself from falling down. She clung there for a moment and then shouted back, angrily:

'They ain't no Albert! They ain't no Albert! That's somebody I made up. They never was no Albert.'

His face appeared suddenly, thin mouth bared, at the kitchen door.

'No?' he said. 'They never was no Albert, wasn't they?'

'No, they ain't no Albert! I made it up –'

'I seen you!' he shrieked. 'I seen you up there! I seen you! – I bin watching all afternoon! – I bin watching!'

She saw the gleam of the shotgun barrel as he whipped it from behind the door with the air of violently conjuring it from nowhere. She slipped in her new shoes on the carpetless stairs as she ran. She began to sob again that there was no Albert, that it was only a name, a someone she had made up, and then a shot blasted the stairs and the landing, spraying the walls and the woodwork as she slipped in her new shoes for the second time.

It was the slip of her shoes that kept her down under the high trajectory of the shot. She fell against her bedroom door, opening it at the same moment, and threw herself inside. The second shot roared up the stairs, shattering the ceiling this time so that a hail of rotten plaster fell on the stairs and the bricks of the narrow passage below.

She locked the door and then pressed with all her weight against the long old-fashioned bolt, ramming it into place with a rattle that was like the echo of the second shot. In the act of doing this she used her ungloved hand and then she remembered the glove that had fallen from the table to the kitchen floor.

She began to cry. The recollection of the glove she had lost seemed suddenly more painful and more bitter than anything else that had happened. She lay face downwards on the bed in her new clothes, clenching with one gloved and one ungloved hand the edges of the canopy, sobbing with bitterness into the pillow, her face dark in terror.

From outside she heard the staggering crash of Parker as he lumbered up and down the stairs.

'You never thought I see you, did you?' she heard him yell. 'You never thought I could see you – well, I see you, I see you – plain as daylight, you bitch!'

The word had the effect of pinning her down, in final paralysis, to the bed. It terrorized her more than the sound of the third shot, fired wildly across the landing with echoes of broken glass.

'You hear that?' he yelled. 'That's what bitches get! That's what you'll get too, you bitch – I can wait for you!'

She had nothing to say in answer. He fired a fourth shot and she heard it rake along the bones of the ceiling, bringing down a fresh hail of plaster.

'Y'ain't got nothing to say now, you bitch, have you? Well, it don't matter! – I can wait as long as you do. I can wait – I'm going to shut your mouth for you. I'm going to shut it for a long time. I can wait for you!'

She lay on the bed all night, not moving. Sometimes she heard Parker staggering about the house, yelling her name. There was no sound of another shot. In the deep darkness she could not sleep, but she cried from time to time as she remembered the glove she had dropped in the kitchen below. Then gradually her thoughts mounted and became an obsession about the glove, scared and fixed and predominant, and of how, sooner or later, by some means or other, she must go downstairs and find it again and go away.

11

SOMETIMES if the wind was right she could hear the chimes of the church clock coming up from below the hill and all through the next morning she lay on the bed and counted the hours by the strokes coming faintly through the quiet October day. Then she heard the ringing of bells for morning service and she knew that when they stopped it would be eleven o'clock. She still did not move as she listened to these things. Her thoughts remained obsessed, fixed always on the glove she had dropped and how, when two o'clock came, she would have to bring herself to face the business of unlocking her door and going downstairs and finding the glove and going away.

After the bells had stopped ringing for morning service, an enormous quietness came down across the hill. She found herself listening for sounds of Parker. It seemed strange not to hear the sound of a rusty cow-stall hinge and the clank of a half-door thrown back against a wall. It was odd that there were no sounds of cow-hocks whispering in straw or padding down through the flint yard to lower pastures. The mornings were always so full of these noises that they were as natural to her as the rising sun.

It was the deepening of this curious silence that made her turn over at last and lie on her back and listen more intently. It was strange that there was no sound of cows or feet in the yard, but it seemed stranger still that there was no sound of Parker. She thought of this for a long time. Then she began to think over Parker's habits and she remembered that he had a Sunday morning habit of cleaning his boots in the shade of the bullace-tree that hung over the hen-house across the yard. He liked to sit there for two hours or more spitting on the toe-caps of his boots and rubbing spittle and polish round and round with his fingers. The hens would cluck about him, scratching in the straw, and towards dinner-time she would take him a jar of cider and a glass and he would sit there drinking and polishing for another hour. That too, like the sound of waking and walking cattle, was as natural to her as sunrise.

Towards midday she got up for the first time and looked out of the window. It was possible to see the hen-house from the window of her bedroom but she saw at once that there was no Parker there and that the hens had not been let out for the day. There was no stir of anything about the bullace-tree except a blackbird attacking one of the fallen fruit as it might have attacked a snail, knocking it from side to side with its beak and exposing the raw green-yellow flesh. She saw then that the cow-barn had not been opened either and as she listened for the noise of animals moving she was aware of the silence amplifying and deepening all across the hillside in the late October sun. It seemed to cover everything with a soft close curtain and once again the wide low valley did not seem large enough to contain the deep discharge of her feeling, her fear that Parker was waiting, her joy at the thought of the young man, a profound cold wonder that such a thing could ever have happened to her. Then as she stood there she became aware, suddenly, of an extraordinary lessening of her fear. It was exposed as baseless in a flash that arose from a sudden twist in her mind.

'Because if I'm late he can come down all the way to meet me,' she thought. 'Then I'll be able to see him from the window. Then I can wave to him and he'll come down and nothing can happen.'

Her reassurance about this was so complete that she began to get herself ready. In her mind the solution to things fell into place as simply as her scheme about the exploitation of Parker and Parker's passion for her and Parker's money had once fallen into place.

She stripped off her clothes. Her body was moist and creased from her night on the bed and her hair was pressed into a waveless mass that fell untidily about her neck. She washed her body as she had done the previous day, drying herself slowly, and then carefully putting back her clothes. She felt again the heavy pulse of satisfaction at seeing her body, coarse and floppy when naked, grow gradually into something that became smooth and silky and beautiful as she covered it with the corset, the stockings and lastly the dress and the shoes.

This transformation seemed even deeper with her hair. She combed out the waves, wetting them with the tips of her fingers and setting them back into place. During all this time, about an hour, she listened for the sound of Parker and for the sound of the church clock striking the quarters from below the hill, never hearing the one but always the other, her fear lessening and her confidence growing at the same time.

When finally she was ready she stood in front of the glass again, turning sometimes to see if the seams of her stockings were straight, touching the waves of her hair, thinking how wonderful it was that her legs and her hair were not as they used to be, thinking how much of herself was different.

'I'm all different,' she thought. 'He said I was. You're different somehow and I don't know how, he said.'

Just before two o'clock she stood at the bedroom window, watching the track that came down along the edge of the wood. She drew on her one glove slowly, remembering at the same time how she must pick up the other.

After a few moments she saw the young man coming down under the edge of the beeches. He had put on a new brown tweed jacket and she felt her heart give a pained start of joy, almost a stab, because he had dressed himself in his best clothes to come to meet her. She saw him come down past the point where he had dusted her shoes and she had taken him into the wood because her eyes were dazzled by the sun. She could see him with wonderful clearness and she knew then the reason for that strange stark feeling of nakedness the previous day. It was her own queer premonition that Parker was watching her.

Thinking of Parker, she listened for a final sound in the house. When she could hear nothing she opened the window. The young man was standing about two hundred yards away, waiting for her, and she began to wave her hands. At first he did not see her and suddenly she had a violent impulse to shout to him. She wanted to call his name. Then she remembered that she did not know his name and she felt herself framing the name Albert soundlessly with her lips instead.

Suddenly he saw her and began to wave his hand. She threw up her own hands in a great double gesture of beckoning, repeating it excitedly. He seemed to understand what she meant and began to walk down towards the farm, baring his teeth as he laughed and waved his hand.

A moment later she pulled back the bolt of the bedroom door and then turned the key and opened the door and stood on the landing outside.

She began trembling again as she saw the shattered bones of the ceiling and the mess of fallen plaster and its dust on the stairs. There was still no sound in the house. With a great breath she stiffened and found all her courage and called:

'Mr Parker! I'm going now, Mr Parker! I'm saying goodbye now, Mr Parker. I'm going home.'

She waited a second or two for an answer that did not come and then she walked downstairs, crunching over fallen plaster.

At the door of the kitchen she stopped again. 'Mr Parker,' she said. 'I don't want to cause nobody no hard feelings but I'm going now, Mr Parker. I'm going home.'

Parker was not in the kitchen. There was no sound in the house. Then suddenly she saw her glove lying on the floor of the kitchen, under the table, where she had dropped it the previous day.

She forgot about Parker as she ran and picked it up.

All her life with Parker and her fear of him seemed remote and pointless in the moment of finding her glove. She felt quite calm again as she drew it on. She even found herself taking a final look at her hands, their coarseness hidden at last by the clean white kid, before she walked out of the kitchen for the last time.

She had hardly walked a dozen yards from the house before she heard the shot. A hundred yards away the young man threw his hands to his face and then clawed them away again, as if wrenching something from his eyes.

She was aware of wanting to scream his name. Then she remembered for the second time that she did not know his name and her mind began to scream 'Albert! Albert! Oh! my God, Albert!' though her lips did not utter a sound.

Above and behind her, from the top of the house, she heard a yell from Parker. She turned and saw him with the barrels of the shotgun levelled on the rails of the little balcony. She screamed again but the sound of her scream was shattered by the blast of the second shot. She saw the young man blown backwards in the act of wildly trying to wrench the pain from his eyes and then his body, convulsive like a rabbit's, turn over and at last lie still.

'Oh! my God, my God,' she said. 'Oh! Albert – Albert – Oh! my God.'

She stood still for a moment longer, weeping. Then she began to run, raising her white gloves in agony against the sky.

More about Penguins

Penguinews, which appears every month, contains details of all the new books issued by Penguins as they are published. From time to time it is supplemented by *Penguins in Print*, which is a complete list of all available books published by Penguins. (There are well over three thousand of these.)

A specimen copy of *Penguinews* will be sent to you free on request, and you can become a subscriber for the price of the postage. For a year's issues (including the complete lists) please send 30p if you live in the United Kingdom, or 60p if you live elsewhere. Just write to Dept EP, Penguin Books Ltd, Harmondsworth, Middlesex, enclosing a cheque or postal order, and your name will be added to the mailing list.

Note: *Penguinews* and *Penguins in Print* are not available in the U.S.A. or Canada

Laurie Lee

CIDER WITH ROSIE

Recalling life in a remote Cotswold village nearly forty years ago, Laurie Lee conveys the semi-peasant spirit of the England we have traded for the petrol engine.

'This poet, whose prose is quick and bright as a snake ... a gay, impatient, jaunty and in parts slightly mocking book; a prose poem that flashes and winks like a prism' – H. E. Bates in the *Sunday Times*

AS I WALKED OUT ONE
MIDSUMMER MORNING

It was 1935. The young man walked to London from the security of the Cotswolds to make his fortune. Then, knowing one Spanish phrase, he decided to see Spain. For a year he tramped through a country in which the signs of impending civil war were clearly visible.

Thirty years later Laurie Lee has captured the atmosphere of the Spain he saw with all the freshness and beauty of a young man's vision.

'A beautiful piece of writing' – John Raymond in the *Observer*

A ROSE FOR WINTER

Fifteen years after his last visit to Andalusia Laurie Lee returns.

He finds a country broken by the Civil War, but the totems of indestructible Spain survive: the Virgin in agony, the thrilling flamenco wail ... the pride in poverty, the gypsy intensity in grey slums, the glory in the horror of the bullfight, the exultation in death, the humour in hopelessness ... the paradoxes deep in the fiery bones of Spain.

The Go-Between

L. P. Hartley

'Of all the novels L. P. Hartley has written I think *The Go-Between* is the best ... it is in what is to me the best tradition of fiction' – John Betjeman in the *Daily Telegraph*

In one of the first and finest of the post-war studies of early adolescence, an old man looks back on his boyhood and recalls a summer visit to a Norfolk country house at the beginning of the century.

Not yet equipped to understand the behaviour of adults, he is guiltily involved in a tragic drama between three grown-up people. The author forcefully conveys the intensity of an emotional experience which breeds a lasting mistrust of life.

The Wild Cherry Tree

H. E. Bates

In each of these ten stories H. E. Bates evokes places and defines a life you could never before have imagined. A pig farmer's wife secretly builds up a 'rich, expensive, dazzling' wardrobe to escape the filthy squalor of her life; a hypocritical do-gooder is driven to more than distraction by two Jaguar-belt sirens; a woman wearing odd stockings gets involved with a man who reads his newspaper upside down...

The Wild Cherry Tree shows Bates at his most tense and immediate; observing with baleful accuracy just what happens when people are 'thrown suddenly with neither direction nor compass into territory utterly strange or unexplored'.

H. E. Bates

THE WEDDING PARTY

A collection of thirteen short stories ranging from the humour of *The Picnic* and *Early One Morning* to the tragedy of *The Primrose Place* and the drama of sorrow and beauty of *The Wedding Party*.

Each one is a slice of life – your life.

A MOMENT IN TIME

She was still in her teens when they came to fight a war in the air. Day by precarious day she shared with these dedicated youngsters – hardly more than boys – dangers unbearably heightened by the peace of the English country-side.

THE DISTANT HORNS OF SUMMER

James's new nanny was seventeen years old and almost as innocent as he was. Life was good together. She entered into his imaginary world. She made friends with his invisible 'mates', Mr Pimm and Mr Monday. Then Mr Ainsworth came along. From the very beginning James's new nanny gave more attention to him. It was enough to make a boy leave home . . .

FAIR STOOD THE WIND FOR FRANCE

'Perhaps the finest novel of the war . . . The scenes are exquisitely done and the characters – tenderly and beautifully drawn – are an epitome of all that is best in the youth of the two countries. This is a fine, lovely book which makes the heart beat with pride' – *Daily Telegraph*

NOT FOR SALE IN THE U.S.A.